Taste Bud Pledge

"I promise to keep my mind open and my fork ready, to try each new food at least two times, and to share what's on my plate when someone doesn't have enough."

To my mother, for teaching me to appreciate food and family by forbidding books at the dinner table, while encouraging my imagination to wander by pretending not to notice my reading light on after bedtime. —S.T.

To my boys—Brock, Jude, Ollie, and Rusty—and of course to my dad, whose gifts in the kitchen set me up for a lifetime love of food. —J.K.E.

Copyright © 2021 by Kalamata's Kitchen, LLC
Illustrations by Jo Kosmides Edwards

All rights reserved. Published in the United States by Random House Children's Books, a division of Penguin Random House LLC, New York.

Random House and the colophon are registered trademarks of Penguin Random House LLC.

Visit us on the Web! rhcbooks.com

Educators and librarians, for a variety of teaching tools, visit us at RHTeachersLibrarians.com

Library of Congress Cataloging-in-Publication Data is available upon request.
ISBN 978-0-593-30791-5 (trade) — ISBN 978-0-593-30792-2 (lib. bdg.)
ISBN 978-0-593-30793-9 (ebook)

MANUFACTURED IN CHINA   10 9 8 7 6 5 4 3 2 1   First Edition

Kalamata's KITCHEN™

Written by **Sarah Thomas**

Created by **Derek Wallace**   Illustrated by **Jo Kosmides Edwards**

Random House 🏠 New York

Nothing seemed unusual in Kalamata's kitchen. Raindrops pattered against the window. The pages of Mama's cookbook made a soft scratching sound as she turned them. The fridge hummed along in a low, steady buzz.

groceries
- [x] turmeric
- [x] garlic
- [x] onion
- [ ] green chilis
- [ ] mustard seeds
- [ ] cumin seeds
- [ ] coconut oil

But tonight was not a normal night at all, because tomorrow would not be a normal day. Tomorrow would be Kalamata's first day in her new school.

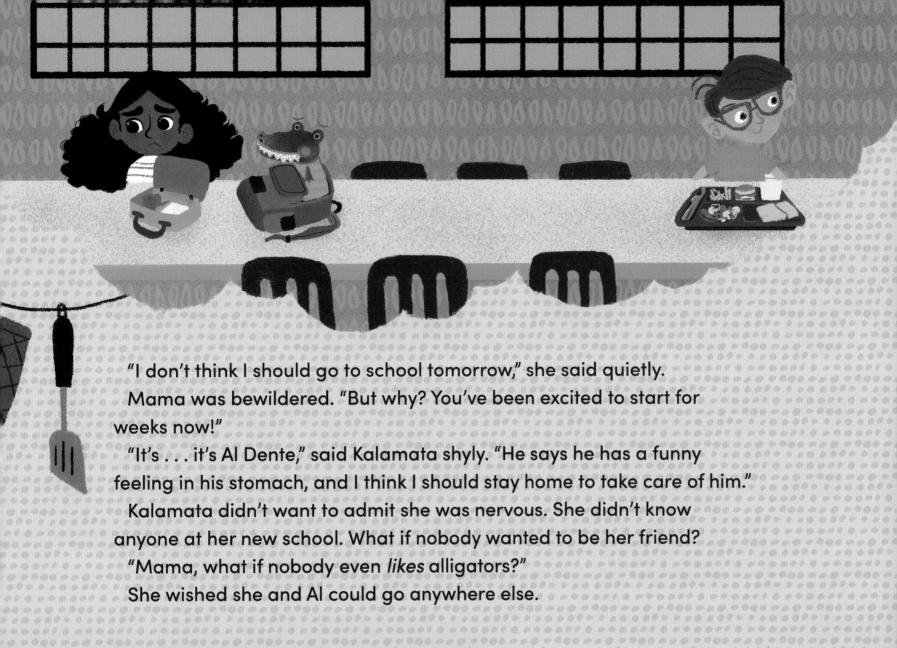

"I don't think I should go to school tomorrow," she said quietly.

Mama was bewildered. "But why? You've been excited to start for weeks now!"

"It's . . . it's Al Dente," said Kalamata shyly. "He says he has a funny feeling in his stomach, and I think I should stay home to take care of him."

Kalamata didn't want to admit she was nervous. She didn't know anyone at her new school. What if nobody wanted to be her friend?

"Mama, what if nobody even *likes* alligators?"

She wished she and Al could go anywhere else.

"Well, what do you think might make Al Dente feel better?" asked Mama.

Kalamata thought about the wonderful trip to India she had taken with Mama and Appa that summer. At first, she had been scared to enter a noisy, busy market. But she had Al by her side, and soon she was dazzled by colors and smells and smiles all around her.

"Al wasn't scared to try ANYTHING in the market! And nobody was scared of him, either. Maybe we should go back!"

"If we went to India right now, we might not make it back in time for school," Mama said as she rummaged through the kitchen cabinets. "Maybe you and Al just need to be reminded that you can be brave!"

CHAI

If only I could find a way to feel brave, Kalamata thought.

A cloud of fragrance whooshed over Kalamata as Mama opened the spice cabinet. The delicious smells made her nose perk up and her mind start to race. For just one moment, all her nerves were forgotten. Could the answer be in her own kitchen *right now*?

Kalamata had to find out. While Mama brought out dried lentils from the pantry, Kalamata grabbed Al Dente and crawled under her kitchen table.

Grown-ups never
seemed to notice, but
Kalamata's table was
magical. Under her table,
she and Al Dente could
transport themselves
anywhere.

Tonight, she was going back to the spice market. She just had to close her eyes and take a deep breath, and then something magical would happen. . . .

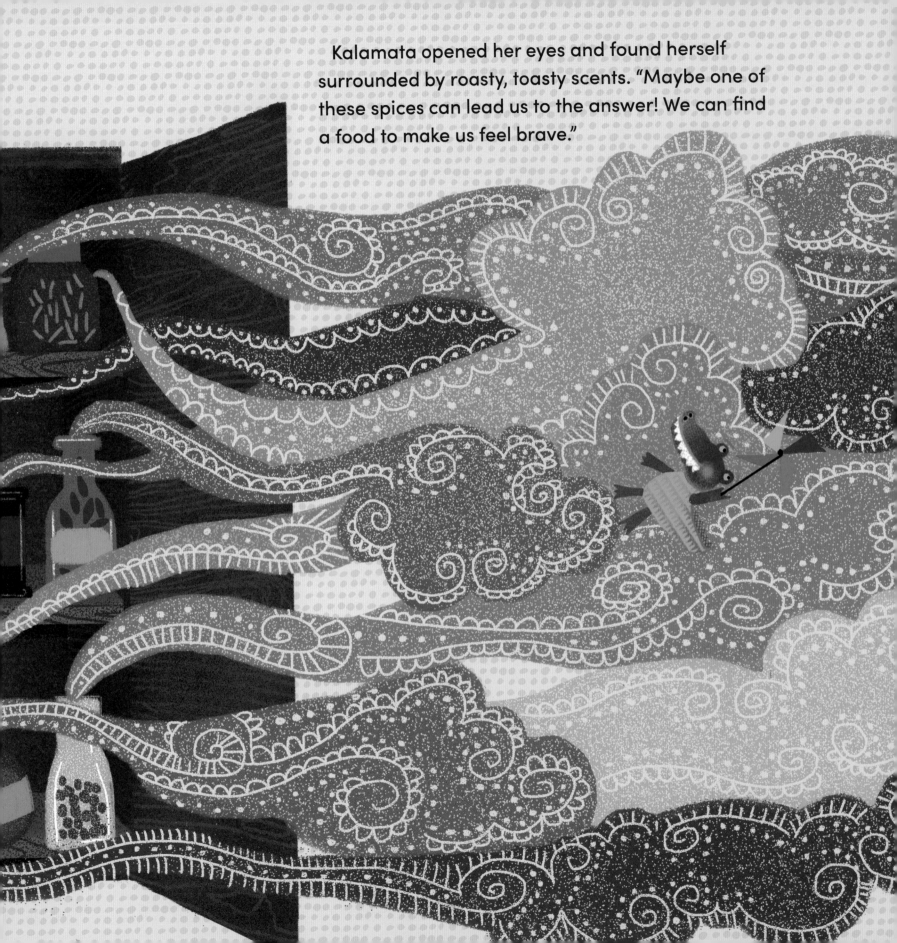

Kalamata opened her eyes and found herself surrounded by roasty, toasty scents. "Maybe one of these spices can lead us to the answer! We can find a food to make us feel brave."

A wave of cinnamon tickled her nose. A *poof* of chili powder made her tongue tingle. Rich curls of cumin warmed her from the inside out.

"What if we could live in this smell forever, Al?" she wondered.

The spice wind blew them to the peak of a mountain of dazzlingly yellow turmeric. "A clue!" Kalamata exclaimed.

The rush of wind in her hair and the spray of golden turmeric behind her made Kalamata laugh. "Everything in the market was bright and beautiful, so I know this food must be a feast for my eyes and my tummy!"

There was a sizzle in the distance, and the world blossomed into a deep, dense curry-leaf forest. Kalamata and Al Dente climbed to the top of the branches and swung from them.

The sharp, fresh smell of blooming curry leaves filled
Kalamata. "I can almost *taste* the air!" she cried out in
delight. "It's all starting to seem so familiar. . . ."

Loud POP POP POPs filled the sky. Brilliant mustard-seed fireworks exploded above them. As the oil shimmered and spluttered, Kalamata's anticipation grew and grew.

"What if this food even *sounds* like a party, Al?"

As the fireworks glittered and faded,
soft, fluffy flakes of rice fell around her.

She and Al whizzed along, and she tilted her head back to catch a taste.

Suddenly, all the scents, sounds, and sights that surrounded Kalamata seemed to click into place. A rumbly feeling in her tummy had replaced the scary one. This feeling was good. *This* feeling meant it was time for dinner.

"Al, I didn't recognize all these clues before, but I think I've got it now! It wasn't just one food at the market that made us feel brave!"

Kalamata realized that though she had been scared to go to the market, the trip had been a fantastic food adventure. "You know what, Al? Being brave is delicious!"

Kalamata felt triumphant as she crawled out from under her kitchen table.

"Mama, we figured it out!" she announced proudly as Mama slid a bowl of fluffy white rice and bright yellow dal in front of her. She took a deep breath, and the smell and warmth of the dish spread over her face.

She felt *fearless*.

"We all get nervous sometimes," Mama said gently. "Even alligators like Al Dente! He's lucky to have you to remind him how to face what scares him."

As Kalamata dug into her dinner, she
wondered if her new school friends might
be fearless food adventurers, too.
She couldn't wait to find out.

Kalamata's Dal*

*or, as Al Dente likes to call it—Dal-amata!

This recipe for dal is based on one commonly used in South Indian households. In the north, you might encounter creamier versions and different spices. There are endless dal preparations. How many have you tried?

- 1 cup dal (such as split yellow mung beans), rinsed, then soaked for 10 minutes

- 1/4 tsp. turmeric

- salt to taste (roughly 1 tsp.)

You can use as many of these additional ingredients as you'd like!

- 1 tbsp. coconut oil or vegetable oil

- 1/4 tsp. brown mustard seeds

- 1/2 tsp. whole cumin seeds

- 1 tsp. garlic, minced

- 1 tsp. ginger, minced

- 1 small onion, chopped

- 2 green chilis, slit

- 1/4 cup curry leaves, stems removed

- 1 tbsp. ghee

- cooked rice, chapati, or another cooked grain or bread

Place dal and 4 cups of water in a saucepan. Bring to a boil, then cook at medium-low heat for 20 minutes or until dal starts to soften. Stir in turmeric and salt. Cook for another 20 minutes or until dal is soft but still holds its shape. Drizzle ghee on top and serve, or continue to next steps.

Heat oil in a small saucepan over medium-high heat. When oil is hot (it will start to shimmer), add mustard seeds and cumin. As soon as mustard seeds pop, add garlic, ginger, onion, green chilis, and curry leaves. Sauté until everything browns a little and the curry leaves turn a shade darker, about 1 minute. Stir the mixture into the dal. Taste and add salt if needed, and drizzle additional ghee on top for added richness. Serve over rice or other accompaniment.

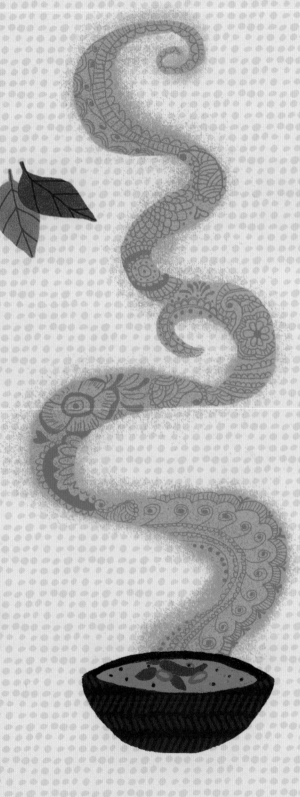

One Last Bite!

Dal: "Dal" can refer to dried lentils and other similar legumes or to food made with them. Many types of dried legumes can be called dal, with endless varieties of the dish all over the Indian subcontinent. You'll find dal as a staple in millions of kitchens around the world because it is easy to prepare, versatile, healthy, and affordable.

Turmeric: Turmeric is one of the oldest-known spices from India, valued for centuries for its beautiful golden color, earthy flavor, and medicinal properties. To make the powder we use as a spice, the roots of the turmeric plant are boiled in water, dried, then ground.

Mustard seeds: Did you know your favorite hot dog condiment comes from a plant? Every part of the mustard plant is edible, and each is used all over the world to enhance different cuisines. In Indian recipes, you are most likely to encounter mustard in its seed form. The seeds don't have a smell until they are bloomed in oil, when they pop and release a strong fragrance that enhances many delicious dishes.

Blooming spices: The additional step of blooming, or tempering, spices in oil gives Kalamata's favorite dal its unique flavor. When spices are heated in oil, they release more intense flavors and aromas. While Indian cuisine varies widely from region to region, this method is shared across the subcontinent. Learn different words for the sizzling of spices on the map!

Did You Know?

There are thousands of languages and dialects spoken around India. Learn what "tempering" is called in just a few!

"CHHONK"
HINDI

"TADKA"
HINDI

"PHORON"
BENGALI

INDIA

"VAGAR"
GUJARATI

"CHHUNKA"
ORIYA

"PHODNI"
MARATHI

"POPU"
TELUGU

"THALIKKA"
MALAYALAM

"THALIPPU"
TAMIL